I Love My Hat

by **DOUGLAS FLORIAN**   *Illustrated by* **PAIGE KEISER**

two lions

One autumn morning, Farmer Brown got on his tractor and headed to town.

Soon he saw a calico cat.
"Nice hat, calico cat!" said Farmer Brown.

"Thanks!" said the calico cat, and he started to sing.

"I love my hat!
I love my hat!
I love my hat!"

sang the calico cat.

"Hop aboard," said Farmer Brown.

Soon they came across a nanny goat.
"Nice coat, nanny goat!" said Farmer Brown.

"Thanks!" said the nanny goat,
and she started to sing.

"I love my coat!
I love my coat!
I love my coat!"

sang the nanny goat.

"Hop aboard," said Farmer Brown.

Soon they came across a big white ox.
"Nice socks, big white ox!" said Farmer Brown.

"Thanks!" said the big white ox,
and he started to sing.

"I love my socks!
I love my socks!
I love my socks!"

sang the big white ox.

"Hop aboard," said Farmer Brown.

Soon they came across a pig in the sty.
"Nice tie, pig in the sty!" said Farmer Brown.

"Hop aboard," said Farmer Brown.

Soon they came across a field mouse.
"Nice blouse, field mouse!" said Farmer Brown.

"Thanks," said the field mouse, and she started to sing.

"I love my blouse!
I love my blouse!
I love my blouse!"

sang the field mouse.

"Hop aboard," said Farmer Brown.

Soon they came across a pig in the sty.
"Nice tie, pig in the sty!" said Farmer Brown.

"Thanks," said the pig in the sty, and he started to sing.

"I love my tie!
I love my tie!
I love my tie!"

sang the pig in the sty.

"Hop aboard," said Farmer Brown.

Soon they came across two turtledoves.

"Nice gloves, turtledoves!" said Farmer Brown.
"Thanks!" said the turtledoves, and they started to sing.

"I love my gloves!
I love my gloves!
I love my gloves!"

sang the turtledoves.

"Hop aboard," said Farmer Brown.

Soon they came across a big brown bear.
"Nice underwear, big brown bear!" said Farmer Brown.

"Thanks!" said the big brown bear, and she started to sing.

"I love my underwear! I love my underwear! I love my underwear!"

sang the big brown bear.

"Hop aboard," said Farmer Brown.

Soon they came across two caribous.
"Nice shoes, caribous!" said Farmer Brown.

"Thanks!" said the two caribous,
and they started to sing.

"I love my shoes!
I love my shoes!
I love my shoes!"

sang the caribous.

As they pulled into town, the animals sang,

"Farmer Brown, you need new clothes! Dress yourself up from your nose to your toes!"

"Off I goes," said Farmer Brown.

And when he got back, he sang a song.

"I love my clothes!
I love my clothes!
I love my clothes, wherever I goes!
I love my clothes,
    when the autumn wind blows!"

To my cousin, Marilyn Miller
—D. F.

For Marcia
—P. K.

two lions

Published by Two Lions, New York

www.apub.com

Amazon, the Amazon logo, and Two Lions are trademarks of Amazon.com, Inc., or its affiliates.

ISBN-13: 9781477847800
ISBN-10: 1477847804

The illustrations were rendered in watercolors, brush and ink, and pastels on soft press watercolor paper.

Book design by Abby Kuperstock

Printed in China
First Edition